I need a NEW BUTT!

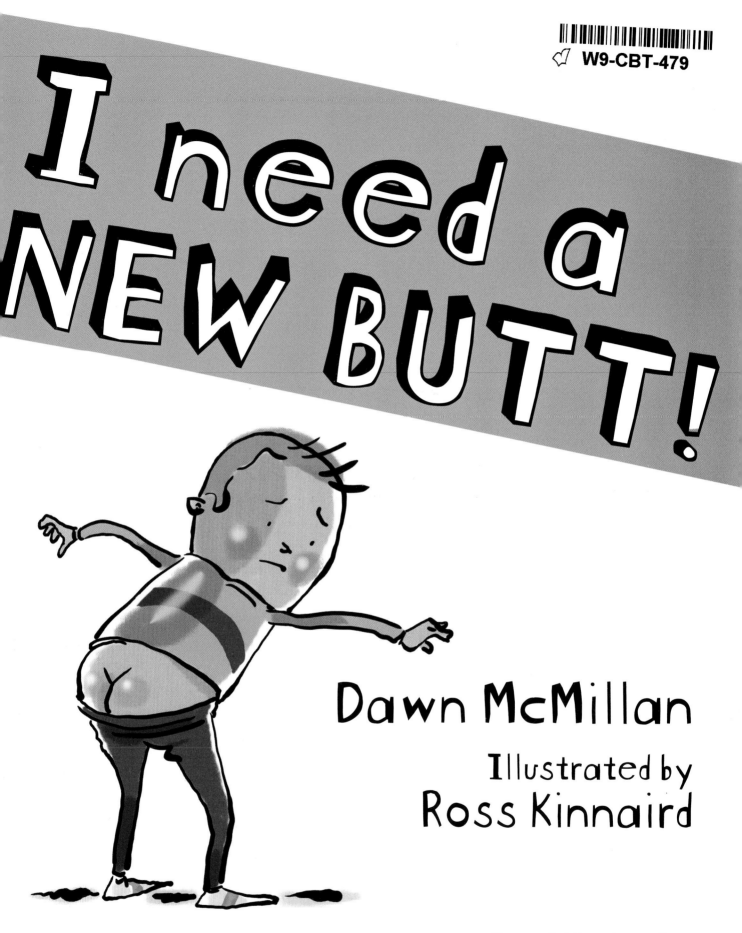

Dawn McMillan

Illustrated by
Ross Kinnaird

Dover Publications, Inc.
Garden City, New York

I need a new butt! Mine's got a crack.
I can see in the mirror a crack at the back.

Did I do it on the slide?

Or on the banister inside?

Or when I jumped my BMX?
Or with the fart? That happened next.

Of course! The fart!
That's what blew my butt apart!
Split the thing clean in two.
Now I wonder what to do.

I need a new one.
A green one or a blue one.

A fat one or a thin one.
A wood one or a tin one.

Why not an **arty-farty** butt?
One not to be forgotten,
with watercolors on the top
and a mural on the bottom.

Or ...
yellow spotted?
Purple dotted?

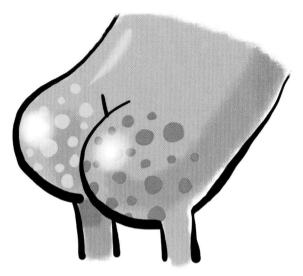

A butt with color.

A butt with flair.

A butt as **bright** as I dare to wear.
A butt as bright as ...

... Dad's underwear!

Or maybe an alien's butt,
made from a metal
like titanium.

Fireproof!
Bulletproof!
Bombproof!

I'd like a butt that's safety-rated.
The right butt …

a knight's butt …
a butt that's **armor-plated**.

What about …
a bumper butt
made of chrome?

Why not, I say,
from a 1960s sport coupé,
one made in the USA.

With accessories to complement,
like strips of silver smoothly bent,
a set of lights left and right
for backing 'round in the night.

With a bumper butt I won't be scared
because bumper cracks can be repaired.

But ...
a bumper butt is huge!
A bumper butt **weighs**
a ton.

I've changed my mind ...
I want a lighter one.

A rocket butt?
All fire and thrust.

A robo-butt?
Now that butt's a must.

No ... I think it's all too late.
This cracked butt
is my
fate.

I'm here on my own
in this cracked butt zone.
No one to care.
No one to share ...

Wait!
What's that I hear?

This is outrageous!
Are butt cracks contagious?

And Dad …
there's no way of knowing
just how
far
it's
going!

About the author

Hi, I'm Dawn McMillan. I live in Waiomu, a small coastal village on the western side of the Coromandel Peninsula in New Zealand. I live with my husband Derek and our cat, Josie.

I write lots of different things: fiction and non-fiction, poetry, stories for school readers and stories for picture books. Sometimes my work is serious, sometimes it's just for fun. Every now and again I write a really crazy story — this is one of those! Enjoy!

About the illustrator

Gidday, I'm Ross Kinnaird. I'm an illustrator and a graphic designer and I live in Auckland. When I'm not illustrating a book, or being cross with my computer, I enjoy most activities to do with the sea. I love visiting schools to talk about books and drawing. (I've been known to draw some really funny cartoons of the teachers!)

Originally published by Libro International, an imprint of Oratia Media Ltd, 783 West Coast Road, Oratia, Auckland 0604, New Zealand (www.librointernational.com).

ISBN-13: 978-0-486-78799-2
ISBN-10: 0-486-78799-0

Manufactured in the United States by LSC Communications
78799020   2020
www.doverpublications.com